Gabby
Enjoy the Book.
M. L. Russell

Binky the bunny's winter tale

Hannah Russell

This book is dedicated to my brother John
- Thank you for letting me play with all your toys at Christmas time when I was younger because I thought they were better than mine x

Once upon a time...

It was the night before Christmas and the animals where getting ready for the big day ahead.

Mighty the mouse loved drinking hot chocolate during the winter months it kept him warm when it was cold outside.

Mighty the mouse

Although Christmas day was so close,

there was still lots to do.

Gilbert the Goose had to get a move on

and

deliver his presents to Mighty the

mouse, but getting across the lake was

difficult in winter!

He grabbed his skates and set off on

his way...

Gilbert the Goose

While Gilbert the goose skated across the

lake, Sophie the Squirrel sat by the fire and began to

wrap her presents for her woodland friends.

This year she had got some handmade items from Frankie the fox.

Sophie the Squirrel

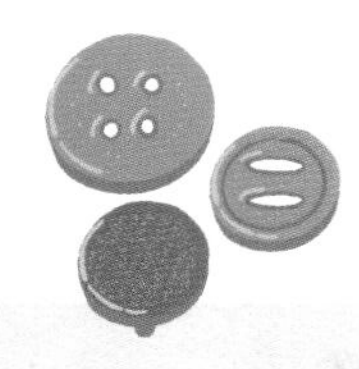

Fiona the fox loved knitting by the fire,
she was making one last stocking to hang up...

Frankie was usually in bed a sleep by this time
but she could hear bramble the bear snoring
from next door.

Fiona the fox

Bramble the bear was listening to Christmas music in his rocking chair when he had fallen asleep.

The excitement for Christmas was just to much for him, he loved seeing all his friends on Christmas day but was most excited about the presents he might receive.

Bramble the bear

Ronnie the Reindeer and Maggie the moose where sat supping mulled wine after prepping the vegetables for tomorrow.

They couldn't wait to see everyone and enjoy Christmas day.

It was only when they stopped talking that they could hear something close by...

Ronnie the Reindeer
Maggie the moose

Bow, Binky and bumble the three bunnies where practicing Christmas carols outside in the village and spreading some Christmas magic when they spotted something fly above...

'Could that be him?' Bumble asked?

'I'm not sure, It's moving very quick' Bow said.

'I think we better get you both to bed or nobody will be visiting tonight..' Binky said as they hopped away..

Bow, Binky &
Bumble the bunny's

All was quite in the woodlands village, you could only hear the sound of a gentle breeze flying through the trees...

Calvin the cat was sat on the fire when he heard something tip toeing on the roof, he jumped in to a stocking to hide from the noise when he thought he saw somebody move across the room...

Although he wanted to stay awake he soon fell asleep and somebody moved him back to his bed while they scattered presents across the floor....

Calvin the cat

The next day on Christmas morning, the woodland friends woke up to stockings full of gifts, bow, binky and bumble where delighted to see they had a small layer of snow on the ground and Bumble hopped between the trees when he noticed an unusual track on the ground..

He followed the track and saw it lead up to the roof tops and a small path of glitter trailed behind.

'Look at this Bow!' He shouted.
Bow came hopping over but as she
reached Bumble the track had
disappeared in a gust of wind and
Bumble was left wondering if he really
had seen it after all.......

The End x

About the Author

Born in the Yorkshire Dales, Hannah's first book was published when she was just 17 years old. Hannah Russell best selling author had success with her series of books based on 'Little Alf" her miniature Shetland pony. Since then Hannah has gone on to write a series of different stories and often includes animals in the books due to having over 20 pets herself.

Find out more online -

Social channels

@hannahrusselllittlealfandfriends

Website

www.hannahrussellauthor.co.uk

Hannah & Bumble the bunny

Hannah has always had a love for bunny's and guinea pigs, over the years she has had a variety of rescue bunny's and guinea pigs...

Muffles x

Malibu x

Merry Christmas Everyone x

Book Publsihed 2021

Printed in Great Britain
by Amazon